THE
CREEK

by Elizabeth Hahn

Illustrated by Katherine Ace

ROURKE PUBLICATIONS, INC.

VERO BEACH, FLORIDA 32964

CONTENTS

Library of Congress Cataloging-in-Publication Data

Hahn, Elizabeth, 1942-
    The Creek / by Elizabeth Hahn.
      p.   cm. —(Native American people)
    Includes index.
    Summary: Examines the history, traditional lifestyle, and current situation of the Creek Indians.
      1. Creek Indians—Juvenile literature. [1. Creek Indians. 2. Indians of North America.] I. Title. II. Series.
    E99.C9H27 1992   976.1'004973—dc20   91-25774
                                                                            CIP
      ISBN 0-86625-393-9   AC

INTRODUCTION

The Creeks originally were called the Muskogee. They lived on lands that now form the states of Alabama and Georgia. When the English settlers arrived, they noticed that the Muskogee built their homes beside creeks and rivers. The newcomers gave the name Creeks to these Muskogee Native Americans.

By the middle of the 16th century, people from England, France, and Spain were exploring the New World. They found fertile farm land and plenty of fish and game, truly a "land of plenty." The Spanish also believed that there was gold to be discovered in this new land.

These three powerful European nations engaged in a race to see which of them could claim most of the New World. It happened that the Creek lands were situated right in the middle of the territories that each of the three foreign nations had staked out. The Spanish approached from the south, where they had extended their colonization from South and Central America into Mexico and Florida. The French had come in from the north to claim eastern Canada and the Mississippi River Valley. And the English had established seaboard colonies from Massachusetts to the Carolinas.

The Creeks were one of the most powerful native tribes in North America. They were not one single tribe but, rather, a group of independent tribes that had banded together in a confederacy. The Creek Confederacy included more than 50 towns in a wide geographic area.

It was only natural that the three foreign powers in North America each wanted to count the powerful Creeks as their allies. From the earliest days, however, the Creeks formed strong alliances

(Photo courtesy of Historical Pictures Service)

with the English. They liked trading with the English, and continued the friendly relationship with them for many years.

The Creeks remained loyal to their English allies during the American Revolution. Only when it was certain that the British were going to withdraw their claims to America did the Creeks sign a treaty with the Americans. The Americans did not easily forgive the Creeks' loyalty to England. They demanded all the territory that now comprises the state of Georgia as payment from the Creeks. Still, it was not enough. White people demanded more and more land from the Creeks as white settlements grew in the South.

The Creeks rebelled, but suffered yet another crushing blow in the Creek War, at the end of which they were defeated in the Battle of Horseshoe Bend (1814). The United States' price for peace was more land—22 million additional acres of Creek territory. Then in 1830, Congress passed the Indian Removal Act by whose terms the Creeks were moved west of the Mississippi River. Within ten years, all Creeks had been forced off the lands where they had lived for centuries.

This is the story of the Creeks.

The CREEK

THE CREEK

THE SEMINOLE

Mound Builders

THOMAS Jefferson was one of the first Americans to try to solve the mystery of the great mounds. These are the sometimes huge monuments made of earth that have been found throughout the central, southeastern, and parts of the western United States. In all, almost 100,000 mounds exist. Some of them are in the form of giant, flat-topped pyramids that are larger even than the Great Pyramids in Egypt. Others are shaped like animals: bears, birds, turtles, deer, and serpents that stretch over acres of land. Today, it is easy to see the shapes from an airplane, but in Jefferson's day, it was much more difficult to distinguish them. The mounds were sometimes mistaken for ordinary hills because they had been abandoned for such a long time.

The first mounds were discovered accidentally by farmers who were trying to plant crops on the hills. They uncovered artifacts buried in the soil. Archeologists—scientists who excavate and study the remains of old cultures—

began to work with Jefferson to find out who had built the mounds and why. The scientists came to believe that the mounds were constructed by Mayan Indians who had traveled from Central America and Mexico into North America in search of better farmland on which to grow their most important crop, corn. These native people from the south would have had to encounter the native people of North America. Scientists believe that these two groups of people did, in fact, meet, and that they merged with minimal struggle.

The North American natives were not agricultural people. They were hunters who depended on fish and game for their survival. The Mayans introduced their northern neighbors to corn. Learning to plant and harvest the crop gave the hunters a more dependable supply of food.

Archeologists believe that the original Mayan settlers were workers, not nobles or priests, because they brought crafts and building skills to North America—not the writing and arithmetic skills that belonged to the upper classes. These early Mayan settlers made jewelry out of polished stones. The jewelry is similar to the necklaces made much later by the Creeks, further evidence that the Mayans were the ancestors of the Creeks. The Mayans were also skilled at making pottery, another craft that they carried with them to their new land. And for some time after their arrival in their new northern home, they continued constructing the same kinds of mounds that they had built in Central America and Mexico. Archeologists believe that building the mounds was the Mayans' way of pleasing the spirits.

Each mound is believed to have been built by hand. Scoops of earth were piled on top of each other until the giant forms were shaped. Sometimes the dead were buried in these mounds. Other mounds contain no human remains or artifacts, leading researchers to believe that they were built as temples. Mayan priests climbed to the top of the mounds to be closer to the sun, which the Mayans worshipped as a god.

At some point, all mound building ceased. No one knows why. But the mound-building people remained. They shared their way of life and many of their myths and legends with their new North American friends, including those that would be the ancestors of the Creeks.

Origins of the People and the Clan System

The Creeks believed that the universe is made up of three worlds: This World, the Upper World, and the Lower World. They described This World as an island suspended from the sky on four ropes. Each rope is attached to the island at one of the four points of the compass: north, south, east, and west. The Creeks believed that a supreme being called the Master of Breaths created all life—people, animals, and plants—in This World.

The Upper World, as the Creeks imagined it, was an ideal place of extreme order and stability. The Lower World was just the opposite. It represented extreme chaos and changeability. The place called This World was physically located between the perfect order of the Upper World and the chaos of the Lower World. The Master of Breaths expected the Creeks to create a balanced life by avoiding the extremes found in both the Upper and Lower Worlds.

The most important factor governing a Creek's daily life in This World was the clan system. The system identified each individual's origins and defined his or her place in the tribal structure. A Creek always was born into a particular clan, the members of which were all related through the female side of a family. A Creek was loyal to his or her clan above anything else in life. Loyalty to one's clan even took precedence over loyalty to one's village. Members of the Deer clan, for example, felt closer to other members of the Deer clan in a distant village than they did to neighbors in their own village who belonged to a different clan.

The clan directed many important matters in life. Even revenge had a code prescribed by the clan system. Revenge was an important matter to the Creeks, and was essential for all offenses, from an accidental incident to murder. If a person was murdered, his or her clan had to avenge the victim. A blood relative had to kill the murderer. If the actual murderer could not be killed, a member of his clan could be killed in his place. Seeking revenge could sometimes take years, but the matter was never closed until the crime was avenged. There were some cases where a clan member volunteered to be killed in place of the real murderer, just to resolve the matter once and for all and lift the shame from the guilty clan.

How the clans came into being was set forth in an ancient Creek legend:

When the Master of Breaths created the first Creek people, the land of This World was covered with a dense fog. It was impossible to see anything beyond a few feet. The people living in This World had to stay together to survive, but they also had to venture away to hunt for food. In their misty surroundings, the people's search for food quickly took them out of each other's sight. As a precaution against becoming separated from the group, these early people devised a special system of calling out to one another. Many of these sounds imitated the calls of animals and birds. And it was

only from hearing such sounds that the people knew of the existence of neighboring groups of people.

After a great while, an east wind came to blow the dense fog away. The first group of Creeks who were able to see the land clearly became known as the Wind Clan. As the east wind continued to blow, more groups of Creeks became visible. When they looked about, they saw land, water, and many different kinds of animals. Each of the groups adopted the first animal they saw as the symbol of their group or clan.

To this day, Creeks identify themselves first as belonging to a clan—the Deer, Turtle, Bear, or Beaver Clans, to name just a few. Then they identify themselves by the particular tribe to which their clan belongs. Each tribe is made up of many different clans.

The legend about the early Creeks also provides some important insight into why the Creeks came to develop a confederacy. Just as the early people lost in the legendary fog had to maintain contact with one another to insure their survival, the clans and tribes of later Creeks banded together in a confederacy to protect themselves from enemy tribes. Eventually, the Creek Confederacy became one of the most powerful groups of Native Americans in U.S. history.

The Creek Confederacy

The Creek Confederacy was a group of tribes that lived in more than 50 different settlements, called *Creek towns*, that spread over a wide geographic area. The settlements were small, but a few had populations of more than 1,000. Some of these villages were referred to as white and others as red. The peace-loving clans lived in "white" villages, and the warrior clans lived in "red" villages. Each village had its own chief. The chief, called a *mico*, was always a man. Periodically, the confederacy held intertribal council meetings at which the micos from all of the tribes met to discuss issues concerning all Creeks. This council also decided if and when the Creeks should go to war. If war was decided, the council elected a war chief to lead the tribes. The war chief was always a member of a red clan. During a war, red and white clans stood side-by-side to fight the enemy. After a war, the peace talks always took place in a white village.

Historians are not exactly certain of when the confederacy was formed, but European settlers who came to the New World in the 16th century reported that leagues of Native Americans already existed.

The Creek Confederacy grew continually. Every time it won a battle, its council offered the losers an opportunity to join the confederacy. Many accepted. By the time the confederacy reached its height, it had approximately 20,000 members.

The connection between tribes in the confederacy was further strengthened by the clan system. With all members of the same clan respecting each other as brothers and sisters, there was a strong bond between members of the same clan, even if they lived in different villages.

Nineteenth century rendering of a Creek tribal meeting.

(Photo courtesy of Historical Pictures Service, Chicago)

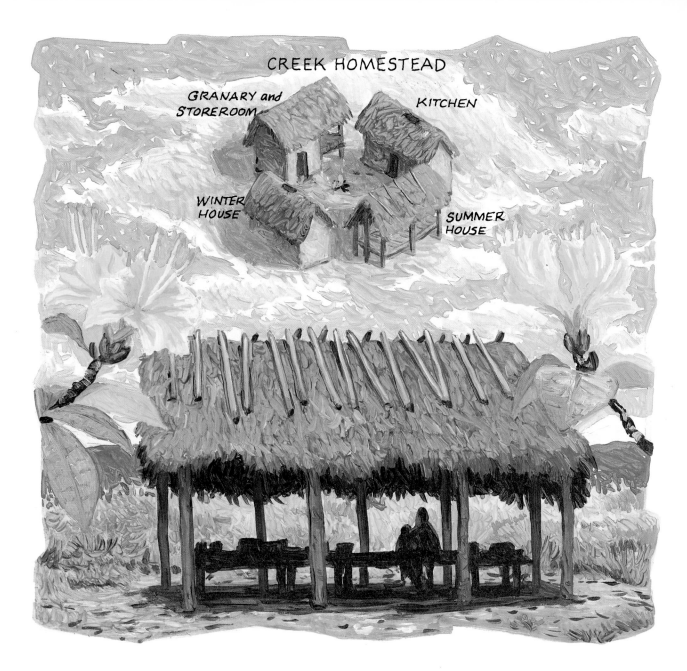

CREEK HOMESTEAD

GRANARY and STOREROOM

KITCHEN

WINTER HOUSE

SUMMER HOUSE

Villages

Creek villages reflected the Creek style of life. When the Creeks were not at war, their life revolved around farming, hunting and fishing, and game playing. At the center of each village was a playing field. Around the field, the Creeks built their houses and council buildings. Beyond the houses were great planting fields.

The playing field in the center of each village was used for special festivals such as the Green Corn Ceremony and for games. In the center of the field stood a 40-foot-tall pole. It was used as a target for archery and spear throwing. Smaller poles in the field were often decorated with scalps and other war trophies.

Several types of houses were built around the playing field. All Creek families had a summer house and a winter house. The summer houses were very open—just four poles supporting a thatched roof to make shade from the hot sun. Winter houses, on the other hand, were completely enclosed. Walls were built by first driving a series of posts into the ground. The Creeks then wove split saplings from pole to pole. The saplings were coated with six or seven inches of a clay and grass mixture to make a stucco-like wall covering. Larger saplings were placed across the top of the walls as beams to support roofs made of cypress bark.

The winter houses had no windows and only a small door. There was a smoke hole in the roof to allow smoke to escape from the fire inside. The Creeks kept a fire going night and day for heat and cooking. The houses, in fact, were so warm that the Creeks wore little clothing inside. The only furniture in these houses were platforms for sitting and sleeping. They were built a few feet off the ground and were covered with mats of deerskin and beaver fur.

A Creek village also included an enclosed round house for winter council meetings. During the warm months, council meetings were held outdoors under large thatched roofs that provided welcome shade from the hot sun.

Beyond the circle of houses lay the planting fields. Farming, especially raising corn, was an important occupation of the Creeks. Fields were planted by the women, and women and children tended the crops. They raised beans, pumpkins, and squash, as well as corn. Corn above all was central to Creek life because it could be dried and stored to insure food for the winter months if the hunts were not successful.

The women were talented farmers. Over the years, they kept developing newer and better strains of corn to improve its nutritional value and durability. They had three basic varieties of corn: red, yellow, and blue. Corn was so important that the Creeks created their calendar year around the planting and harvesting of this crop.

Hunting and Fishing

Farming may have been the mainstay of their life, but the Creeks lived also by fishing and hunting. They fished in fresh-water rivers and streams, using spears, floating traps, and lines with hooks to catch the fish. The Creeks who lived along the coast stood in salt water ponds and speared the fish or shot them with a bow and arrow. They also dug for oysters and clams along the shoreline.

The Creeks were very adept hunters, killing small game and birds with their bow and arrows, traps, and blowguns made from cane branches. The most important animal to hunt, however, was the deer. Its meat provided food and its skin was used to make clothing and blankets. The Creeks' deer-hunting tactics were similar to the Plains Indians' tactics for hunting buffalo. The Creeks often disguised themselves under the skin of a whole deer, just as the Plains Indians hid under a buffalo skin. That way, they could creep closer to their prey and kill it.

Other times, the Creeks might set fire to part of a forest to flush the deer out into the open. Also like the Plains Indians, the Creeks prayed and made offerings to the gods for a good hunt. To guarantee a lifetime of abundant game, they prayed, too, for the continued rebirth of the deer they had killed.

Games

Games were almost as important to Creek life as farming, hunting, and fishing. The location of the playing fields—in the center of each village—attests to the significance Creeks attached to games. Games were hardly ever just frivolous play. Most of them taught the Creeks valuable, life-sustaining skills, and they were practice for real combat. Sometimes the games were almost as bloody as an actual battle. One stickball game was even called "the little brother of war." It was a team sport similar to our modern game of lacrosse. Every player carried two sticks, each 2-3 feet long with a deerskin pocket at one end. The game was played with a ball made of animal hair rolled up tightly and wrapped in deerskin. The sticks were used to toss the ball between players until they got close enough to fling the ball through goalposts set up at either end of the field. The fields were more than 200 feet long, and the action was notoriously wild. Players could use any means they could devise to get the ball to the goalposts. They charged into one another as they tried to snag the flying ball, thinking nothing of bashing their opponents on the head with their sticks, or shoving them to the ground and running over them. Horrible injuries and even deaths often resulted from such brutal tactics. When this game was played between neighboring villages, there could be 75 to 100 men on each team, and as many as a thousand people might show up to watch and cheer their favorite team.

(Photo courtesy of Smithsonian Institution)

Creeks playing a stickball game.

Another game—though much less violent—was chunkey. It was played with a stone disc or hoop that was about a foot in diameter. This game was played by only two men at a time. One player hurled the disc so that it rolled down the chunkey field, which could be up to 100 yards long. Then the thrower and the other player, each carrying a long, spear-like stick with a crook at one end, raced down the field after the disc. While running, each player threw his stick to the place where he thought the rolling disc would come to rest. The object was to have the disc stop rolling in the crook of the stick, a maneuver that took a great deal of skill. The player whose stick came closest to the spot where the disc came to rest was the winner.

Games for girls were not at all violent, but they also had a purpose. They were meant to help prepare young girls for later adult life. Girls played mostly with dolls, pretending the dolls were their babies. Such playing was intended to teach girls how to care for future real babies. Other times, girls played house, where they practiced how to be home-makers like their mothers.

Family Life

Marriages were arranged by the older women of the tribe, and could take place only between members of different clans. Though all of the negotiating was done between the older women, the final decision was the bride-to-be's to make. The first step was for a young man to express an interest in a particular young woman, but he could not speak to her directly. He had to ask one of his maternal aunts to approach one of the young woman's maternal aunts. She, in turn, would find out whether the young woman's family was receptive to such a marriage. Neither the boy's nor the girl's fathers were part of the decision-making process, but they were kept apprised of the negotiations.

If both families agreed that the match was a good one, it was up to the young woman to make the final decision. But she did not give a mere yes or no

answer. She had to perform a formal ritual in giving her reply. One morning, at an agreed-upon time, the girl would set a bowl of hot cereal outside the door of her house. The young man then requested permission to eat the cereal. If the young woman denied him permission, it meant that she did not want to marry him. If she agreed to his partaking of the cereal, it meant she was willing to marry him.

Before the wedding, the young man had to prove his manhood by building a house for his bride-to-be. Then, he had to kill a deer to provide the young woman with food and with skins for clothing. For her part, the bride-to-be had to give the young man an ear of corn or some other food that she had cooked to prove her own worth. This exchange of gifts was all that there was to the wedding ceremony. The married couple then lived together for a year. If at the end of the year either of them had second

Creek men could have more than one wife. If a man wanted to take a second or third wife, he had to ask the first wife's permission, but rarely did the first wife say no. A man's having more than one wife was common and acceptable among the Creeks. A Creek woman, however, could have only one husband. And if a wife was discovered to be unfaithful to her husband, her ears might be cut off as punishment.

Children were highly valued and respected among the Creeks. They began to assist with the adults' responsibilities as soon as they were old enough to walk. All child-raising was done by the mother or her brothers. This followed the Creek belief that bloodlines were carried on the mother's side of the family. A child's father had his own bloodline responsibilities to fulfill: he taught his sisters' children.

Girl children learned to help with the cooking, gardening, pottery-making, basketry, and fire-tending. Young boys, taught by their uncles, learned how to hunt for food and how to fight wars. By the time they were four years old, boys were given small bows and arrows with which to practice. A boy was considered a child until he earned a war title by performing some heroic deed in battle. The war title—a name such as Fights Like A Bear—was a description of the heroic feat. The descriptive title became the young man's new name. It was officially presented to him in a special name-giving ritual at the next Green Corn Ceremony. After that the young man assumed all rights and privileges of an adult in the tribe, including being entitled to attend council meetings.

thoughts about the marriage, they were free to leave with no bad feelings. But regardless of whether the husband stayed or left, the house he had built for his bride was hers to keep.

17

Clothing

The Creeks, living in what is now the southeastern part of the United States, wore little clothing. Most of the year, the climate in that region is warm, if not hot and humid. Men wore breechclouts and, sometimes, a grass blanket over one shoulder. A breechclout, or breechcloth, is a square of deerskin hung from a strip of rawhide around the waist. On special occasions, men wore feathers in their hair.

Women wore deerskin skirts and a grass shawl over their right shoulder. Children went without any clothes until they were 12 or 13. Then they dressed the same as adults.

During the winter months, Creek houses were so hot from the continually burning hearth fires that the people did not have to wear any more clothes than they did in the summer. Creeks went barefoot unless it was very cold; then they wore moccasins. Men also wore moccasins when they had to walk a great distance to another village or when they went to war.

The Creeks covered their bodies from head to toe with paint and tattoo designs. Warriors' tattoos noted their rank in the community as well as their wartime accomplishments. If a warrior decorated his body with a tattoo design he had not earned, he was forced to remove the tattoo. Tattoos were created by pricking the skin with porcupine needles dipped in natural dyes. It was a painful process to undergo—and twice as painful to have a tattoo removed.

Women, too, had tattoos. Their designs represented their tribal status and also their husband's status.

Body painting was a far less painful way for the Creeks to decorate their bodies. The Creeks used certain colors and patterns to paint their faces. As was the case with tattoos, body paintings indicated a man's status and the town he was from. The mico, for example, painted half of his face red and the other half black for ceremonial occasions. For everyday wear, micos painted only a black circle around one eye and a white circle around the other.

Village Government

Village chiefs—the micos—were powerful men, but they did not force rules upon their people. The mico was chosen by the leaders of the village, and those leaders had a definite say in their government.

The leaders of the village, in turn, were chosen by the villagers, who might select any wise man to be one of their leaders. Most often, however, leaders were chosen from strong warriors, medicine men, and priests. These appointed leaders formed a village council, which discussed everything that affected the village, such as planting, hunting, or war plans. The council's ultimate goal was to achieve consensus—to have every member in agreement. If this was not possible, the majority ruled, but no one was forced to agree or punished if he did not agree.

Osceola, Chief of the Florida Seminole people.

(Photo courtesy of Historical Pictures Service)

The Green Corn Ceremony

One of the village council's greatest responsibilities was to organize the annual Green Corn Ceremony. This ceremony, known as a *puskita*, was the most important ritual in Creek life. The rite was probably carried into North America by the ancient mound-building Mayans who migrated from the south. The Green Corn Ceremony was both a religious ritual and a tribal dance, or stomp. It was held in honor of corn, "the grain of life," and the sun. The ceremony, held annually at harvest time, lasted four days.

As the ceremony began, women laid

tree branches on the dance ground around a ceremonial fire, which represented the sun for the Creeks. Before taking part in the ceremony, the men had to purify themselves with the "black drink." Brewed from holly leaves, this drink made the men vomit to cleanse their bodies. This cleansing of the body symbolized the Creeks' desire to purge themselves of past wrongdoings. The purified men then began a dance that lasted throughout the day and night. As the men stomped around the sacred fire, they whooped and shouted and waved tall lances in the air. The lances always had scalps, trophies from past wars, tied to the ends. They were intended to look like the corn stalks that the ceremony was honoring. The men sang and prayed to give thanks for the harvest and to ask for plentiful future harvests.

In between rounds of dances, name-giving ceremonies were held, the ritual in which young boys received the official name that marked their entrance into adulthood.

On the last day of the Green Corn Ceremony, the sacred fire was extinguished. The men scattered the ashes and started a new fire. Custom demanded that the new year's fire be started with seven different kinds of wood. The people prayed for good health and strong alliances in the coming year. All problems and wrongdoings from the previous year were to be forgotten and forgiven so that the new year could begin afresh.

A Creek brave surrounded by the mythic symbols of his tribe.

Warfare

The Creeks were known for being fierce and aggressive fighters. To them war was serious business, and it was never begun without a meeting of the inter-tribal council. If the council decided to go to war, it then chose a warrior to lead the campaign.

A big part of a war chief's duty was to organize the fighting force. War parties were made up of volunteers only. No one was forced to fight. The warriors came to the chief's village to prepare for battle. They spent three days fasting and cleansing themselves with the same "black drink" that they used to purify themselves for the Green Corn Ceremony. As the warriors fasted, older men told the young braves war stories—mostly tales of their own great past victories. Chanting and war dances followed to raise the warriors' fighting spirits. Finally, the warriors painted themselves red and black, their traditional colors of warfare. They were then ready for battle.

The war chief led his party on the warpath. He carried a sacred bundle, a packet filled with objects that the Creeks considered gifts from the gods. The bundle might include parts of a snake and the bones of a panther. The Creeks attributed great powers to these animals, believing that they could help fend off enemy spears and arrows. The warriors marched to battle single file. Each man carefully stepped into the footprints of the man in front of him so that it would look as if only one person—not a whole war party—had walked on the path. This precaution was taken to insure a surprise attack, the warriors' greatest advantage.

Once at their destination, the warriors surrounded the enemy camp, maintaining contact with one another by calling out to each other with imitation bird and animal cries. The attack began on a predetermined signal. First, the warriors rained arrows into the enemy camp. Then, armed with war clubs and spears, they charged, screaming and howling, upon the stunned enemy. With luck, the battle might be over in minutes.

When they were victorious, the Creeks took scalps as war trophies, and sometimes they also cut off an enemy warrior's head to bring home to celebrate their victory. Captives also were taken. Some would be offered positions in the confederacy. Others, not so fortunate, would be made slaves. Still others, particularly if they were feared warriors, would be tortured to death.

After the triumphant warriors returned home, they went through another three days of fasting and purification. To the Creeks, shedding blood was a kind of pollution. If they engaged in it, they also believed that they needed to purify themselves of it. War and the preparation for war were important parts in Creek life.

Fields of Battle

Before the arrival of Europeans in the New World, the Creeks warred only with other Native American groups. These skirmishes had been relatively infrequent, fought mainly over boundaries and the protection of hunting grounds. After the European settlers arrived, the Creeks found themselves increasingly involved in armed struggles.

Of the three European powers fighting for dominance in the New World—England, Spain, and France—it was the English who won the friendship of the Creeks. The Creeks liked trading with the English and believed that they could learn much from these foreigners in their midst. As firm friends of the English, the Creeks first fought against the Spanish. Beginning in 1670, when the English established a colony in Charleston, South Carolina, the British funneled guns to the Creeks and encouraged them to use the new weapons against the Spanish. Then from 1703 to 1708, the Creeks helped the English fight both the Spanish and the French in the Apalachee Wars. Later the Creeks sided with the English in the American Revolution (1775-1783). The American victory in that war brought growing encroachment of white people on Creek lands—and punishment of the Creeks for their support of England in the Revolution. The United States demanded a large land settlement from the Creeks as the price of war.

With ever-increasing inroads into their territory, the Creeks rebelled by launching the Creek War in 1813. The struggle ended bitterly the following year, however, when General Andrew Jackson defeated the Creeks in the Battle of Horseshoe Bend, fought on the Tallapoosa River in what is now east-central Alabama. The Creeks lost yet more land after that conflict. About two-thirds of the remaining Creek territory—what now is the state of Georgia—was taken by the U.S. government.

The Seminole tribe, a southern branch of the Creeks located in Florida, rose up against the United States' annexation of Creek lands. They fought the First Seminole War from 1816 to 1818, a bloody conflict that was continued in the Second Seminole War, begun in 1835. But the tide of history was against the Creeks. After seven more years of desperate fighting, the southern Creeks were all but wiped out. The few who managed to escape hid in the great Florida swamps. All other survivors moved west of the Mississippi River where the U.S. government, in the 1830s, established reservations, large tracts of land set aside as the new home for Native Americans.

Andrew Jackson, seventh president of the United States.

Healing Plants

In their years of bloody warfare and in their violent games, the Creeks sustained many wounds. They devised ways of treating these injuries and illnesses. The Creeks believed that herbs and plants were important instruments for healing, and they used them cleverly and wisely. In their view, the Earth provided natural ways to heal wounds and to cure sickness and disease.

Cures found in nature were passed from generation to generation of Creek healers. Holly was used to create a brew for purifying the body. Other plants were crushed to extract the juices that provided soothing medications such as morphine and the less potent salicylic acid. Morphine is a drug still used to alleviate pain, and salicylic acid is the main ingredient in today's aspirin compounds. The Creeks also brewed many different kinds of teas from the roots, branches, and leaves of plants and trees. These teas were used to relieve indigestion and other stomach disorders, as well as numerous ailments.

Famous Creeks

Chief Tuscalusa was one of the first Creeks to encounter Hernando De Soto and his Spanish army. In 1539, De Soto and his forces marched into Tuscalusa's village and paraded about on their horses. The Spanish considered Native Americans savages and wanted to impress them with their power. De Soto asked Tuscalusa to announce his arrival among other Creek tribes so that they could prepare a proper welcome for the Spanish forces. Tuscalusa pretended to agree, but instead of passing on De Soto's instructions for a festive greeting, he warned the Creeks in a town called Mabila to be prepared to defend their stockaded town against the Spanish. The town was located north of the present-day city of Mobile, Alabama.

The unsuspecting Spaniards marched into Mabila where some Creeks welcomed them with singing and dancing. But suddenly, a Spanish soldier noticed several armed Creek warriors hiding on rooftops. He alerted De Soto and a battle ensued. Anticipating an assault, Tuscalusa and his warriors had come to help the people of Mabila, and together they were able to drive the Spaniards out of the town.

Outside the stockade, however, it was a different story. On the open ground, the Spaniards used their horses to trample the Creeks. The Creeks' wooden spears and arrows were no match for Spanish swords and guns. The Spanish drove the Creeks back into Mabila and set the town on fire. Tuscalusa led his people in a heroic defense, but the flames eventually got the best of them. More than 2,500 Creeks died in the battle, but they had let the Spanish know that they were prepared to fight fiercely to protect their lands.

Chief Tomochichi and his ten year old nephew, Tooauahowi.

Chief Tomochichi was another great Creek mico. His village was on the site of what is now Savannah, Georgia. He was a wise leader who believed that his people could learn much from the British settlers. When the British arrived, Tomochichi negotiated a friendly relationship between the Creeks and the newcomers. Then in 1734, General Oglethorpe, the Englishman who had received a charter from King George II to settle the colony of Georgia, invited Chief Tomochichi and his wife and ten-year-old nephew, as well as six other Creek chiefs, to London to meet

Chief Tomochichi and his delegation negotiate a treaty with a bewigged King George II and his ministers.

with King George II. The Creeks were treated with respect, and a mutually agreeable treaty was negotiated between the Creeks and the British. When Tomochichi and the Creeks returned to America, they shared the news with the rest of the Creek Confederacy, and the Creeks lived in harmony with the English until the time of the American Revolution.

When Chief Tomochichi died in 1739, General Oglethorpe saw that he was buried with full military honors. He also ordered a monument to be built in his honor, and it can still be seen in Savannah today.

Alexander McGillivray, a Creek military leader and diplomat, was the son of a wealthy Scottish trader who had married the daughter of a Creek chief. The young McGillivray was raised in a Creek village until he was 14, and then was sent to the British city of Charleston, South Carolina, to be further educated. He grew up to be a strong, clear, and respected voice for the Creek nation.

During the American Revolution, he represented the Creeks in their alliance with the British until it became clear that the British were going to lose. Then, through skillful negotiations, he signed a treaty with the Americans on behalf of the Creeks. This Treaty of New York, signed in New York City in 1790, was the first formal agreement between the Creeks and the new U.S. government. The Americans wanted to foster a friendly alliance with the powerful Creeks, so they made the skillful negotiator, McGillivray, a brigadier general in the U.S. Army. At the same time, the Spanish, who were concerned about their lands in Florida, also offered the well-known McGillivray a high position in their army. McGillivray accepted both positions for his own benefit and for the benefit of his people. Somehow, the Spanish never saw him in his American uniform, nor did the Americans ever see him in his Spanish uniform. McGillivray continued to deal with both governments to his people's best interests until the time of his death in 1793. In the years that followed, the fortunes of the Creeks deteriorated tragically.

The Creeks Today

In the 1830s, after the U.S. government passed the Indian Removal Act, the Creeks were forced to move to Oklahoma. Only a few—approximately 500 Seminoles—stayed behind by hiding in the great Florida swamps. Today, their descendants can still be found in remote parts of the Florida Everglades.

Those Creeks who were moved to Oklahoma tried to pick up some of the good aspects of their life and start again. By the Indian Removal Act, the government allotted large tracts of land—reservations—to the Creeks so that they could build new villages and plant new crops in Oklahoma. For a period, the U.S. government also allowed the Creeks to have their own tribal government. At this time the Creeks established a school, Bacone College, still in existence today as a fully integrated college.

But this reestablishment of Creek life was not to last. When the Civil War broke out in 1861, many Creeks volunteered to fight for the South. In all, more than 11,000 Native Americans fought with the Confederate Army. Unfortunately, just as they had chosen the losing British side during the American Revolution, the Creeks again allied with the side that would lose in the Civil War. The Creeks fought heroically and were one of the last fragments of the defeated Confederate Army to surrender. Nonetheless, in being allies of the losers, they had to give up some of their reservation lands as part of the price of war reparations. Within ten years, the U.S. government took vast amounts of Creek land to allot to other Native Americans who also were being forced to move to Oklahoma.

The Dawes Act of 1887 further depleted Creek land holdings as it divided the Oklahoma Indian Territory into small parcels and required all Native Americans living there to accept individual tracts of 160 acres each. Then

(Photo courtesy of Creek Council House Museum)

Creek Council House shaped like a Mayan pyramid. Scientists now think that the Creeks were influenced by Mayan architecture.

The buffalo dance is performed at a tribal meeting.

Pakoska Billy, a pure-blooded Muscogee, or Muskogee, shows off a plate of pelofu tafum pece (bottom onions). Creeks used five different types of wild onions in their cooking.

in 1889, President Benjamin Harrison opened the Territory of Oklahoma to white settlers for homesteading, and they took over much of what had been tribal territory.

The Curtis Act of 1898 formally abolished all rights of tribal governments, preparing the way for Oklahoma statehood in 1907 and for the assimilation, or Americanization process, of all Native Americans in Oklahoma.

Not until the Wheeler-Howard Act was passed by the U.S. Congress in 1934 did the Creeks have the right to restore their tribal governments. But it took another 34 years, until 1968, for the U.S. government to restore Creek reservation lands to the tribe.

Today, there are about 15,000 Creeks living in the east-central part of Oklahoma. They have one of the best-organized tribal governments in the state, and Creek leaders participate in the large intertribal council meetings that also include the Cherokee, Choctaw, Chickasaw, and Seminole tribes in Oklahoma.

In addition to their commitment to education, the Creeks work hard to maintain a good health-care system for their people. They administer their own hospital, the director of which is a Creek graduate of Harvard Medical School. Many reservation areas for Native Americans do not have medical facilities as advanced as those of the Creeks.

Other Creeks work to preserve the age-old traditions and customs of their ancestors so that they will not be lost to future generations. Annual powwows—social gatherings or ceremonial meetings—are held on the reservation grounds. Stories are told, stickball is played—much less dangerously than in the old days—and a Green Corn Ceremony is performed. The public is invited to attend the powwows, events that provide an opportunity to learn firsthand about the ancient and colorful culture of the Creeks.

Muscogee, Seminole, and Yuchi men and women play stickball at the Council Oak Ceremony.

Tribe members participate in Council Oak Ceremony stompdance.

The tribe name may be spelled "Muscogee" or "Muskogee."

Important Dates in Creek History

5000 B.C.	According to archeological evidence, corn is first planted and harvested in Mexico by native people who are to become the ancestors of the Creeks.
1539	Chief Tuscalusa is among the first Creeks to encounter the Spanish explorer, Hernando De Soto. The resulting battle in a town called Mabila is a disastrous defeat for the Creeks.
1703-1708	The Creeks side with the British against the French and Spanish in the Apalachee Wars.
1734	Chief Tomochichi goes to England to sign a treaty with King George II, giving the British land to establish the colony of Georgia.
1775-1783	The American War of Independence is fought, in which the Creeks side with the English.
1790	Alexander McGillivray signs the Treaty of New York, the first treaty between the United States and the Creek Confederacy.
1813	The Creek War begins, as the Creek Confederacy votes to resist by force the onslaught of white settlers who blatantly ignore the terms of the Treaty of 1790.
1814	The Battle of Horseshoe Bend is fought. General Andrew Jackson and the U.S. Army demolish the Creek forces, bringing the Creek War to a bloody end.
1830	The U.S. government passes the Indian Removal Act, giving President Andrew Jackson the power to move all Creeks to lands west of the Mississippi River, where they are settled on reservations.
1861-1865	The American Civil War is fought, during which the Creeks fight on the side of the Southern Confederacy.
1887	Congress passes the Dawes Act, leading to the elimination of tribal reservations in Oklahoma. The Creeks and other Native Americans are forced to settle on small individual tracts of land.
1889	President Benjamin Harrison opens the Territory of Oklahoma to white settlers for homesteading.
1898	The Curtis Act is passed by the U.S. Congress, abolishing the rights of all tribal governments, and beginning what the whites refer to as the assimilation, or Americanization process, for all Native Americans.
1907	The Territory of Oklahoma becomes a state.
1934	U.S. Congress passes the Wheeler-Howard Act, allowing Native Americans to reinstitute their tribal governments.
1968	The U.S. government returns ownership of the Oklahoma reservation lands to the Creeks.

INDEX